Alexander, Who's Trying His Best to Be the Best Boy Ever

For Shelly Markham—wonderfully gifted composer, arranger, pianist, and friend
—J. V.
To my lovely wife, Marta Cera
—I. M.

ATHENEUM BOOKS FOR YOUNG READERS
An imprint of Simon & Schuster Children's Publishing Division
1230 Avenue of the Americas, New York, New York 10020
Text copyright © 2014 by Judith Viorst
Illustrations copyright © 2014 by Isidre Monés
For information about special discounts for bulk purchases, please contact Simon & Schuster Special Sales
at 1-866-506-1949 or business@simonandschuster.com.
The Simon & Schuster Speakers Bureau can bring authors to your live event. For more information or to book an event,
contact the Simon & Schuster Speakers Bureau at 1-866-248-3049 or visit our website at www.simonspeakers.com.
The text for this book is set in Plantin Std.
The illustrations for this book are rendered in pen, ink, and watercolor.
Manufactured in China
0614 SCP
First Edition
2 4 6 8 10 9 7 5 3 1
Library of Congress Cataloging-in-Publication Data
Viorst, Judith.
Alexander, who's trying his best to be the best boy ever / Judith
Viorst ; illustrated by Isidre Monés in the style of Ray Cruz. — First edition.
pages cm
Summary: After eating an entire box of doughnuts leads to consequences Alexander does not like,
he decides to be the best boy ever for the rest of his life.
ISBN 978-1-4814-2353-3 (hardcover)
ISBN 978-1-4814-2354-0 (eBook)
[1. Behavior—Fiction. 2. Family life—Fiction. 3. Schools—Fiction. 4. Humorous stories.] I. Monés, Isidre, illustrator. II. Title.
III. Title: Alexander, who's trying his best to be the best boy ever.
PZ7.V816An 2014
[E]—dc23   2013047674

Alexander, Who's Trying His Best to Be the Best Boy Ever

JUDITH VIORST
illustrated by Isidre Monés
in the style of Ray Cruz

Atheneum Books for Young Readers

New York London Toronto Sydney New Delhi

Last night somebody ate a whole box of jelly doughnuts and hid the empty doughnut box under the couch. I'm not saying who that somebody is, but this morning, when I woke up, I had a bellyache.

The good news is, I get to stay home from school. The not-so-good news is, it's Saturday—there's no school. The other not-so-good news is that my mom found the empty doughnut box under the couch, and she's back in my room, and she's shaking her finger at me, and she's got her serious face on, and she's saying seriously, "There are going to be consequences."

Consequences are what you get when you do what you shouldn't have done. I hate consequences.

"What kind of fool eats a whole box of doughnuts?" my brother Nick is asking me. I'm not answering.

"What kind of fool hides a doughnut box under the couch?" my brother Anthony is asking me. I'm not answering.

My mom says that my consequences are staying all day in my room with no video games or watching stuff on TV, even though I'm thinking that video games and watching TV might help make a bellyache get better.

I hate consequences.

My dad says after breakfast he'll take Anthony and Nick on a nice long bike ride.

My mom says when they go biking, she is going to take a nice long bath and a nap.

I ask if that means she won't be playing Go Fish or bingo with me while I'm staying here in my room all day with a bellyache. My mom says while I'm staying here in my room all day with a bellyache, I should think a lot about *how* I got that bellyache.

But instead I'm thinking I should have hid that doughnut box under my mattress or way back in my closet where moms might not look. And while I'm thinking of other cool places to hide an empty doughnut box, I have to go to the bathroom and throw up those doughnuts.

Bleh!

My bellyache is going away, but my consequences are staying. And I'm stuck here, all alone in my room, and I'm thinking. I'm thinking how good it feels when I'm eating doughnuts. And I'm thinking how yucky it feels when I'm throwing up. And I'm thinking how much I love eating jelly doughnuts. And I'm thinking how much I hate having consequences. And I'm thinking I hate those consequences much, much, much, much more than I love doughnuts.

And so, when my dad comes home with Nick and Anthony from their bike ride, and my mom is done with taking her bath and her nap, I tell them I am sorry I ate the doughnuts.

And then I tell my mom and my dad a whole new thought I thought while I was thinking, a whole new thought that sneaked into my head. Starting right now, I tell them, I am not getting into trouble anymore. Starting right now, I am only doing nice things. Starting this very minute I am being the best boy ever for the complete and entire rest of my life.

Nick says, "Yeah, right, lots of luck with that plan."
Anthony says, "Forget about it—no way."

And then my dad says what if I try to be the best boy ever for just one week—counting the rest of today as my first day—and after that we can see about me being the best boy ever for the complete and entire rest of my life.

So beginning right this minute I've stopped wishing my brothers' bikes had gotten flat tires. I'm scraping some melted chocolate out of my drawer. I'm saying about a million "pleases" and "thank yous." I'm picking up stuff I dropped all over the floor.

At bedtime my mom gives me kisses and hugs and tells me that my consequences are over. I tell her no more consequences for me. Because I'm finished with trouble, and I'm trying my best to be the best boy ever.

On Sunday morning I get out of bed very early. I almost—but I don't—turn on the TV. Everyone else is sound asleep, but I'm not waking them up. I'm walking on tiptoes, quiet as I can be. I'm not even bouncing my basketball, though I really want to see if I can beat Anthony's record of ninety-six bounces.

I'm not bouncing my ball because I'm trying my best to be the best boy ever.

Everyone's still asleep, and I'm still walking around on tiptoes. But it's lonesome being awake all by myself. It's boring being awake all by myself. I'm tired of being awake all by myself. And I'm thinking that if I went out the front door and rang the doorbell five, six, seven times, no one would be sleeping anymore.

And I'm thinking that if I started practicing "Sweet Home Alabama" on my guitar, no one would be sleeping anymore. And I'm thinking that if I took all the books off the bookshelves in the living room and built a tower as high as I could reach, and then that tower accidentally came crashing down to the ground, no one would be sleeping anymore.

I don't do any of that because I'm trying my best to be the best boy ever.

On Monday, when I go to school, I remember to bring my homework, which means I'm not in trouble for forgetting it. I also don't talk in class when I'm supposed to not talk in class, even though not talking is hard to do, especially when I need to tell James that three tigers were born at the zoo, and also that he's smelling kind of smelly.

I raise my hand every time Ms. Klimpt asks a question—like who was our first president and how do you spell "receive" and what's forty-seven take away twenty-two—even if I don't always know the answer. And when she looks at me funny, because I'm raising my hand all the time, and asks, "Alexander, is something the matter with you?" I say I'm just trying to be the best boy ever.

Ms. Klimpt is uh-huh, uh-huh-ing me, like I'm telling her I'm trying to be Superman. But I don't care. I'm thinking, *Wait, you'll see.*

So then when she starts to carry this really gigantic plant upstairs to the teachers' lounge, I show her I'm nice by saying *I'll* take it—let *me*.

And I'm thinking Ms. Klimpt
should not be looking as worried
as she's looking when, with
just one little wobble,
I take ahold of it.

So I'm carrying the plant. And I only trip once. And I only bump into three people; maybe four. And I only break off some leaves and also some flowers. And when I get to the teachers' lounge and I set down the plant too close to the edge of the table, and it starts to fall off the table and toward the floor, I—just in time—catch it!

And I'm thinking Ms. Klimpt should be sounding a lot more thankful than she's sounding when she's thanking me for carrying that plant.

On Tuesday I keep on raising my hand, though I think Ms. Klimpt's getting grumpy. I remember to walk, instead of run, down the hall. At our soccer game, I don't start yelling "NO FAIR, NO FAIR, NO FAIR," though I'm absolutely positive I could have scored tons of points if I'd just been given a chance to kick the ball. But I never, not even once, was given a chance to kick the ball, and the other team won by about a thousand to zero, which—if I wasn't trying my best to be the best boy ever—I would have been yelling a lot of "NO FAIRs" about.

At dinner I use my napkin to wipe my mouth, not blow my nose. I even get up and put my plate in the sink. "Look at that little angel," says Nick. "He's such an angel," says Anthony. And they're flapping their arms. And I'm getting real mad. And I think I'd like to pour spaghetti sauce into Nick's lap. And dump the whole bowl of spaghetti on Anthony's head. But even though they keep flapping and flapping while I get madder and madder, I make myself sit and finish my milk instead.

It's not easy trying to be the best boy ever.

I make my bed Wednesday morning without being told to. I brush all my teeth—not only in front but behind. On the yellow school bus, while everyone else is shouting and shoving and teasing, who do you think is being gentle and kind? And who do you think is crawling around on the yucky school bus floor, helping Maisie look for her lost glasses?

When I sit back in my seat, Zack, who's next to me, swings his feet, harder and harder until— by mistake—he clonks me. And I'm thinking I really shouldn't, and then I'm thinking I really want to, clonk him back. Because it hurts where he clonked me. Because I'm guessing it *wasn't* by mistake. And because Zack's swinging his feet again, and I really want to get *him* before he gets *me*.

And I'm wondering if I keep swinging my feet until—by mistake—I clonk Zack, am I trying my best to be the best boy ever?

I swing my feet.

On Thursday, after school, I study guitar at Shelly's Music Shack. My mom comes with me and takes a guitar lesson too. We're working on a song we're playing together at the next Shelly's Music Shack concert. And while we're rehearsing our song, I'm kind of hopping and jumping around like rock stars do. And I think I'm hearing somebody saying I shouldn't. And I think I'm hearing somebody saying, "Watch out." But I keep hopping and jumping until I'm sure I hear someone shouting, "Stop, Alexander!" Except by then I've slipped, tripped, crashed, and kind of messed up Shelly's Music Shack.

And I'm wondering if—by accident—
I mess up Shelly's Music Shack, am I trying
my best to be the best boy ever?

Before I go to sleep I decide
that one maybe-mistake and
one not-on-purpose accident
don't count as not trying.

On Friday, on the school bus, I help Maisie look for her glasses—again.
I sit as far away as I can from Zack. When Andrew pokes me in the side
with his very pointy elbow, I accidentally by mistake poke him back. But I
don't tell Maisie I'm getting tired of helping her find her glasses and that
maybe she ought to tape them to her face, even though (and I know this
isn't nice) I'm absolutely bursting with wanting to tell her.

In class I try not to raise my hand unless
I'm completely positive I really know the
right answers to Ms. Klimpt's questions.
But I still raise my hand too much because I
sometimes don't know if my answers aren't
right. Ms. Klimpt says I'm wearing her out
and that she'll give me extra credit if only I
would please stop raising my hand. And I'm
wondering if I stop raising my hand and stop
wearing Ms. Klimpt out, am I trying my best
to be the best boy ever?

I keep raising my hand.

Tonight Nick and Anthony come into my room and start bouncing on my bed. They grab my arms and get me bouncing too. We're up, we're down, we're up, we're down. We're having so much fun doing what we're not supposed to do.

"What's going on in there?" my mom is calling. "Behave yourselves, boys," I'm hearing my dad say. And because I'm trying to be—well, I guess you know what I'm trying to be—I chase my brothers away, and I stop bouncing.

When I open my eyes on Saturday, the first thought I think is, I've done it—I've been the best boy ever for one whole week. But right after that I'm thinking that trying to be the best boy ever was really *hard*. And right after that I remember that now I'm supposed to start trying to be the best boy ever FOR THE COMPLETE AND ENTIRE REST OF MY LIFE. The complete and entire rest of my life, I'm all of a sudden thinking, is a long time.

For the rest of my life I won't get into trouble. For the rest of my life I'll only do nice things. No clonking. No poking. No bouncing on beds. No messing up music shacks. No waking people up with doorbell rings. For the rest of my life I'll be looking for Maisie's lost glasses. Making sure the back of my teeth are clean. No yelling "NO FAIR" no matter how no fair they're being. No wishing for bad stuff to happen when brothers are mean.

Just thinking about how hard it will be, I'm getting the kind of bellyache I got when I ate that whole box of jelly doughnuts. And I'm thinking I'd much, much rather get a bellyache from doughnuts than a bellyache from being the best boy ever.

And then I start thinking I know a cool place—a really, really cool place . . .

where a person could hide an empty doughnut box.